This book belongs to

____

For Ayla, Freya, and Colter –

who remind me that the smallest moments

are often the most magical.

May the rain always sing to you.

PITTA
PATTA

I can hear raindrops on the roof.

Pitta Patta, Pitta Patta.

Like tiny drums tapping a tune.

Pitta Patta, Pitta Patta.

I can see raindrops on the ground.

Pitta Patta, Pitta Patta.

Like sparkly diamonds in the sun.

Pitta Patta, Pitta Patta.

pitta patta

I can feel raindrops on my head.

Pitta Patta, Pitta Patta.

Like butterfly kisses on my hair.

Pitta Patta, Pitta Patta.

pitta patta

I can taste raindrops on my tongue.

Pitta Patta, Pitta Patta.

Like sipping bubbles from the clouds.

Pitta Patta, Pitta Patta.

I can smell raindrops in the air.

Pitta Patta, Pitta Patta.

Like flowers stretching in the breeze.

Pitta Patta, Pitta Patta.

I can splash in raindrops with my boots.

Splish, Splash, Splosh!

The puddles laugh and dance with me.

Pitta Patta, Pitta Patta.

pitta patta

pitta patta

I can spy the rainbow after rain.

Shiny, Bright, and Tall.

The raindrops fade, but colours stay.

Pitta Patta, Pitta Patta.

Copyright © 2026 Sarah Lynch
Illustration Copyright © 2026 Sanna Sjöström

All rights reserved.

No part of this book may be reproduced, stored in a retrieval system,
or transmitted in any form or by any means, electronic, mechanical, photocopying,
recording, or otherwise, without prior written permission from the publisher.

Published by Little Lynch Books
Melbourne, VIC, Australia
www.littlelynchbooks.com

ISBN: 978-1-7645200-1-0

For press, purchasing enquiries, or other correspondence, please contact:
hello@littlelynchbooks.com

Printed in Australia

www.ingramcontent.com/pod-product-compliance
Lightning Source LLC
Chambersburg PA
CBHW042201030726

47599CB00004B/818